Ten Years
and Nothing

TEN YEARS
AND NOTHING

Latonia A. Nettles

Rev. date: 05/26/2021

To order additional copies of this book, contact:
Xlibris
844-714-8691
www.Xlibris.com
Orders@Xlibris.com
828845

CHAPTER ONE

Terry was different, Shelia felt it at her core. She knew that her being here was a bad idea. She had told herself that showing up at his apartment so early in the morning wasn't wise, but she hadn't slept much the last few weeks, and the sleepless nights were beginning to wear on her.

She just needed to talk to him, to try to understand why he felt like this decision that he had made, was what was right for them. If she could get some clarity from him, maybe, they would be able to work through their issues and mend their relationship.

She asked him again. "Terry, what happened between us?"

It was the same question she had been asking him for the last few months, and she was hoping that this time he could give her something more than just empty words. She prayed that this time he could give her real answers and not just his typical let's-just-be-friends reply.

He looked at her for the first time, staring intensely into her eyes. She couldn't read his face, but she felt that what she saw in his eyes was pity. He didn't answer her, he just stared at her. He was making her uncomfortable. It was as if he was toying with her, making her beg him for answers that she felt he owed her.

She used to love how he looked at her with his deep brown eyes. Just one look from him would leave her feeling like a queen. She used to tell him that his eyes were what initially attracted her to him. His eyes and the way his personality drew her and others around him in. He was definitely a people person, always so confident and ready to make anyone laugh with his silliness.

They had met their freshmen year of college, during an end of semester party in a home of one of their mutual friends. He was tall, much taller than her 5'2" height, and she had loved how she always had to look up at him. He wasn't necessarily muscular, and in fact, she would have even said he was on the slender size for a guy of his height.

When they had first met, he walked up to her and shouted over the too loud music, "Do you want to go somewhere and talk?" She remembered the moment specifically, because the loud music was the only reason why she had agreed to walk out of the safety of the party to stand on the front porch with him. From their first conversation Terry had made her feel seen, and not just for her looks, but she felt like he actually listened to her.

He was charming, polite, a true-gentlemen and funny. She wasn't sure how long they talked that night, but if it had not been for her good friend Lisa, she probably would have stood there all night and all the next day talking to him. After they had said their goodbyes, and Lisa had dragged her to the car, Terry had shouted out to her asking if he could have her number. She had smiled and said yes. That's when they exchanged numbers, and over the next few weeks they had spent every free moment they had either talking on the phone or sneaking off to grab coffee or a quick bite to eat. Trying to balance a new relationship with a full load of classes wasn't easy, but they managed to make it work, and soon their innocent friendship had turned into a monogamous relationship.

Now here they were, at the end of a relationship that had never grown past boyfriend and girlfriend. Yes, she knew they had their issues. What relationship didn't have problems? Still, she had been certain that by now they would have at least been engaged. So certain, that she had been shocked when he had come to her three months prior and ended their relationship. His reason for breaking up with her had made no sense, and over the last three months he hadn't been able to give her a reason that she could live with.

Over the last year of their relationship, it had felt like they had stopped moving forward. She had felt it, but that wasn't reason enough for him to break-up with her. There were other options, she had even suggested that they start doing more date nights together. He, of course, had dismissed the idea and instead of going on dates he had actually suggested they take a break! But she wasn't willing to break up then, and she didn't want to break up now. They were so close to marriage, why couldn't he see that?

Instead of trying to find ways to mend their relationship, all Terry ever talked about was money or his next promotion. When they made love, if they made love, she never felt connected to him. She knew that if they tried to make their relationship work, they could once again be the happy and in love couple that they were before, but Terry didn't want to even try.

He looked away first, staring at a blank spot on the wall. He took a deep breath and paused. Finally rushing the breath out of his body, he closed his eyes and responded, he spoke softly but the words were so loud "I've already told you; we just want different things. We grew apart, and I need more than what you can offer me right now." The same words as before, almost verbatim. She didn't want to hear it; she didn't believe him. After ten years of being together. Ten years of growing together, this is the answer he gives her. There was no closure in his words, only more questions. What was he even talking about? Growing apart? They wanted different things. So, she was the problem? Who was this man? He certainly wasn't the man she was in love with. Why couldn't he be straight forward with her instead of speaking in general terms? If he could be honest with her, tell her what he really wanted, maybe then they could work on fixing their relationship.

She had always wanted the same thing; her feelings had never changed. She only wanted him. To be his wife, to have his children. True, they had problems, but she knew that if he truly wanted to be with her, that they could work through their problems. That's what couples did, they saw a problem, and together they came up with a solution to fix the problem. If only he would just tell her what he wanted.

She shook her head, took a deep breath and realized she

couldn't exhale. Her breath was stuck at the bottom of her lungs.

"I CAN'T" she screamed, not meaning too, but it was the only way for her to release the breath. "I can't", she said softer and more controlled. "I love you so much, I just needed to know, but I can't, I mean I don't understand where this is coming from. I thought we were headed towards an engagement, and now you want to break up with me? Then when I come to you to talk you just keep giving me the same bull crap about changing, well isn't that what couples do, they change and grow together"

Her mind went blank, she didn't know what she wanted anymore. Why was she once again trying to make him want her when it was clear that he no longer did? Why was she still trying to find something when she didn't even know what he was looking for?

"I have to go; I need to go" she whispered with blurry eyes. She begged herself not to cry, she had broken down in front of him the last time she was here and this time she wanted to save herself the embarrassment. Even still she wanted him to ask her to stay. She wanted him to make love to her, to hold her and kiss her, to tell her that they would work through this. Looking into his eyes though, she knew he would not. He wouldn't ask her to stay, he would never ask her to stay again.

She stared into his face, fighting back the tears, and hoping for some type of emotion to cross his face. Any emotion other than the void she saw in his eyes would have made her feel better about coming here. She tried to stand up and leave, but she felt so heavy.

After ten years, he couldn't even give her hope. Ten years of her life and now there was nothing. No closure, no sadness, nothing.

CHAPTER TWO

She could feel herself becoming more and more vulnerable as the seconds ticked away. Why couldn't he see how this was affecting her? Or was it that he saw, but that he no longer cared?

He used to always be so caring and loving towards her. She remembered when her Father had died, how he had been there for both her and her mom. Making sure they were both ok. Staying up late nights with her just talking until she fell asleep. So compassionate and loving then. She remembered when she had rear ended another car, he had left work just to come check on her. Even after she had told him she would be fine and that there was no real damage to her vehicle. He still showed up and stayed with her, he even followed her home to make sure she was ok.

Now this bastard couldn't care less what happened to her. She felt so angry she wanted to break something, but she didn't want to give him the satisfaction of making her act out of character. She wanted him to remember her for her smile, for the love she gave him. She wanted him to remember how passionate and how tender she had been with him. She wanted him to remember only the good times with her.

Finally, after what seemed like a million heartbeats, she found the strength to stand up. It was then that she realized he had been talking the entire time. What was he saying?

"I have to go," she rushed her words out "I just remembered that I have somewhere else I am supposed to be." She looked at him, hoping to feel something, anything other than numb. He reached for her hand to stop her. She flinched, moving away from him. At that moment she had a brief feeling of repulsion, now he reacts, after making her feel so useless and unwanted. The saddened look on his face angered her, his beautiful sad eyes made her want to scream. How dare he try to play the victim now, not after how he had given up on them. She felt like such an idiot, after consistently throwing herself at him, begging him to be with her, now when she is ready to walk away, he wants to stop her!

She didn't have anything else to say to him, she merely shoke her head no, turned and walked away.

She walked out of his apartment, into the mid days sun. It was a beautiful day, cloudy but the weatherman hadn't mentioned rain.

She had planned to ask him if he wanted to go for a walk. They had spent so much of their time together, walking, talking and just enjoying each other. She had thought that maybe the act of walking and talking could take them back to happier times. She was wrong. As soon as he had opened his front door and saw that it was her, she realized how wrong she had been.

She couldn't get the way he had looked at her out of her mind. How had they come to this? Ten years together, all of their adult life building together, and he was willing to walk away with not as much as a glance back. How had she fallen in love with someone that was so cold hearted?

She walked to her car, opened the car door and got in. She didn't check to see if he had followed her out. She honestly didn't care anymore.

Cranking the car, placing it into drive and pulling off she headed towards her apartment. They had never lived together, that should have been her first clue that he had never been serious about them. When he had moved out of his parents' house after college, she had asked him about living together in order for both of them to save money. He had said that he didn't want to be one of those couples that were play married. Why did she believe that crap? Especially coming from the guy that always preached about saving money and building for his future. Ten whole years of her life with him and never even the hint of a marriage proposal, then one day he just didn't want her anymore. She had to admit to herself that even the recent talks of engagement where her doing. He never initiated talks of marriage or engagements, all he ever talked about was his future, and his plans. Now that she thought about it, she couldn't even be sure if he was sharing his future plans to include her, or if he had just been rambling. How had she been so naive?

Looking down at the cars odometer she saw that she was going twenty miles per hour over the posted speed limit. The last thing she needed was another ticket, especially since the last one had just fallen off her driving record. She slowed down and took a deep breath trying to calm her nerves. How had she ended up here, ten years later, more lost than she had ever been? She needed to clear her mind or at least get it to a state where she could think rationally. Right now, the only thing she wanted to do was turn around and head back to Terry's. She wasn't sure why she wanted to go back though, was it to give him a piece of her mind, or was it to fall into his arms, even if it was for one last time.

She pulled the car over into a shopping center parking lot, took a deep breath and finally allowed her tears to flow softly down her cheeks. She noticed that almost as soon as her tears began a light rain started. Lately, it seemed that her life was full of cliches, so how appropriate, she thought, as the rain slowly rolled down her front window.

CHAPTER THREE

Terry was confused. Why did Shelia keep popping back up if she wasn't ready to talk about where they had gone wrong? She didn't want to solve anything, the only thing she wanted to hear was how he wanted her back, and he didn't. How could he want her back? Honestly, he couldn't understand why he had stayed with her for ten years. He had known the relationship was doomed during their sophomore year of college. Maybe, he reasoned, he had stayed because she was convenient, or maybe because he considered her just a friend? He didn't know why he had allowed the relationship to drag on, and he hated reducing her to just a college fling because he honestly did love her, but he also knew that he had given his decision a lot of thought, and more than enough time, and he was now ready to move on. I mean he was turning 30 soon and the last thing he needed was to be stuck in a dead-end relationship.

It had been three months since they had broken up, three months of her calling him at random hours, three months of her showing up at his place and at his job unannounced. Why couldn't she get the hint?

When was she going to move on? He had already moved on and this was honestly the happiest he had been in years. He was enjoying being single, meeting new people, and hanging out without having to answer to anyone in particular. Why couldn't she just leave him alone? Why couldn't she just see that they weren't meant to be together?

It wasn't as if the last ten years of their life had been perfect. All they did was argue about the most childish things. They couldn't agree on anything, she saw life as something that happened, while he preferred to plan for life and have a backup plan in case the initial plan didn't work out. It was as if she believed them both to still be freshmen in college when in all actuality, they were closer to reaching the age of 30 than they were to their college age years.

The first two years they were together, it was amazing. They laughed a lot and became the best of friends. He remembered late night conversations, talks of what they both planned to do after college, and he had even entertained her idea of marriage. Then one night out the blue, during one of their late-night talks, she told him she wanted to drop out of college. That is what sparked their first argument. He didn't understand how someone so smart would throw away a perfectly good opportunity of obtaining a degree. She told him some excuse she had of not feeling engaged by the classes, or was it that she didn't feel stimulated? He couldn't remember how she worded it, but ultimately, she had no idea why she wanted to quit, she just wanted to quit.

After the talks of dropping out of school began, breaking

up and getting back together almost seemed like foreplay for them. He couldn't remember how many times he called it quits, or how many times she called it quits, only to be back together the following week or sometimes even the same night.

He knew he shouldn't have taken her back after the first breakup, but he thought he loved her. Well, no, he knew he loved her. That was the problem, he wasn't breaking up for lack of love. He just knew that they couldn't grow together.

After some persuasion from him she ended up staying in college until her junior year. Then she just quit. She no longer took into consideration his opinion on the matter, she merely stated that college wasn't for her and she withdrew. When he asked her what her plan was, she would never tell him. She would just say "I'm just going to see how things go". That was her reply for everything, when he asked about her five-year plan, when he talked to her about applying for another job, even when he approached her about asking for a promotion at her current job. She didn't put thought into anything, she always just waited to see what would happen, and he knew he couldn't be with someone that just lived life on a whim. That's not how he was raised. His dad and mom were very goal oriented, and he always saw himself marrying someone that was goal oriented as well. Someone that he could plan with, build with, grow with.

I mean her she was this brilliant and beautiful woman, and she had no future plans past marrying him. That made absolutely no sense to him.

When he first approached her a year ago about taking some time apart, she had laughed it off and then accused him of wanting to date other women. She had even come up with some idea of going on one date each week to try to rekindle the relationship. Honestly, what would going on dates solve, and why did women always assume that a man wanting to break up meant he wanted to sleep around with other women? It was never about the sex with him, he needed so much more than sex, he needed to feel motivated by his woman, he wanted to be building towards more than just a marriage.

A year ago, he had brought up the idea of them breaking up so that he could clear his head, and also to see what he wanted from life. Could he continue to date her if she wasn't what he wanted? Could he marry her? When the accusations of him sleeping around started, he stayed because he didn't want to hurt her, and also because he can admit now that he was being immature. When he had brought up the idea of breaking up, he knew that staying together was a waste of time, but he just didn't know how to walk away and not hurt her.

Now here they both were at year ten of their relationship, just as lost and confused as they were their freshmen year in college.

He couldn't deny that she was awesome. She was easy to talk to, encouraging, and she gave the best advice. She was what best friends were made out of. He just knew they weren't meant to be married, and that she wasn't what he saw in his future wife.

One of the many times she had brought up the idea of marriage he had considered it, he had even asked her what she thought marriage was, of course she never gave him a clear answer. He remembered her saying something to the effect of two people working through problems. Was that all life was to her, just a problem that took two people to solve? Other than a problem solver, what else did she want? He wanted a partner, more than just a friend or problem solver. He wanted someone that would be as motivated as he was. Even now she was working at a job that she hated, and she hadn't had a promotion or raise in almost two years. When he mentioned to her about going back to school to finish her degree so she could apply for a better paying job, she always said "things will work themselves out" or "we will get through it together". To him that wasn't the way a wife thought, well not his wife. He wanted to be with someone that made things happen, not someone that waited for things to happen, or someone that needed another person to help solve their problems.

Terry stood up from where he was sitting. He had things to do today, and he refused to sit around thinking and rehashing a conversation that he knew would lead nowhere. Shelia had never been one to listen, that was one of his issues with her, she was so bull headed. Even when she knew that what he was saying was best, she always did the exact opposite. For instance, quitting college, applying to a dead-end job, and moving to a city just to be closer to him. Who uproots their life, with no plan, just to follow someone they were just dating? She even tried to use finances as a way to convince him to live with her. If that wasn't a red flag. If she didn't make enough money to sustain her way of living, what made her think she was ready to start a family? Or did she think living together would be reason enough for him to propose marriage to her?

Terry walked to his window and looked out. He half expected to see her sitting in his driveway. That's how he often found her lately. Sitting there just staring at his place. Scared the crap out of him honestly.

He wished he could help her, but he didn't even know what she wanted.

He saw that it was raining softly. He had a ton of things he needed to take care of today, but he also knew he needed time to process what had just happened between him and Shelia. He decided then that the rain was a perfect opportunity to just take a nap.

CHAPTER FOUR

Shelia knew she couldn't sit in the shopping center parking lot all day, but she wasn't ready to head home just yet.

She placed her car in drive, while at the same time hitting the speed dial button on her steering wheel. She knew it wasn't a good idea to call him, but she just needed to talk to someone.

She listened as the phone rang three times; he answered before the fourth ring. "Hello". The sound of his voice immediately calmed her. "Hi" she replied, "I need to talk, can I come over?"

"Sure." he answered with no hesitation.

"Ok, be there in a few minutes."

Ten minutes later she pulled into the driveway of a townhouse, and parking her car she got out and ran up to the door. The rain had picked up slightly since she had left the shopping center parking lot, and she cursed herself for not grabbing her umbrella this morning when she had left home. She was thankful that his front door had an awning over it which provided some protection from the rain. She knocked softly on the front door and waited.

When the door opened, he replied with a deep voice "Hey,

come in out the rain", she smiled and walked in "Hi Sean, I'm glad you were home, I was around the corner and wanted to see what you were up to." She sat on his couch and tried to look as if she hadn't been crying for the last hour.

"What's wrong, have you been arguing with that asshole again?"

She smiled, loving how considerate his voice sounded. She wasn't sure if she should be honest with Sean, or if she should just lie to him. She really didn't feel like rehashing the argument that her and Terry had had earlier. She had always tried to remain as honest as possible with anyone that she dealt with, but right now she just didn't know if she had the energy to talk about Terry. Still the thought of knowing that Sean was always there for her made her feel loved.

Sean had always been a friend that she could turn to whenever she needed some advice. They had met when he worked at the same call center as her a few years ago and they had become quick friends. He was funny, always making her and their co-workers laugh, and he was so easy to talk to. He was also a true gentleman, he had never tried to push up on her like most other men had, and she always felt so at ease with him.

"No, I haven't seen Terry, I just wanted to hang out for a bit." She hated lying to Sean, especially after all he had done for her, but she didn't feel like explaining to him how she had once again made a fool of herself by showing up at Terry's unannounced. She saw Sean as a big brother, and he had become her sounding board over the last few years giving her the male perspective that she needed. When she thought about it, Sean was one of her best friends. He never judged her, he just listened and provided good and sound advice. He had even helped her look for a second source of income a few years back when she had gotten herself into a jam by maxing out three of her credit cards. She had gone to Terry first, and of course he had lectured her on how important credit was and how she would need to figure this out on her own. Feeling defeated and not knowing who else to talk to, she had ended up calling Sean and he had invited her over to his place. That night, Sean had sat down with her and actually walked her through a plan that would help her to reduce her amount of expenses each month, and he also helped her sign up to become a Waiter food delivery driver. It had taken longer than a year, but after some discipline on her side she was able to get one credit card paid off and closed, was almost done paying off the second one, and had a plan in place to pay the third one off. She had also saved over three months of her expenses so that she would no longer have to rely on credit cards.

She could honestly admit that she truly cared for Sean and she appreciated all the advice he had given her over the years, even still she couldn't be honest with him right now.

She knew he could tell that she was lying, but just like the good friend he was, he wouldn't push her to talk about it until she was ready. So instead of asking again, he changed the subject.

"If you say so, do you want to watch a movie; it looks like a bad storm may be coming in. The weatherman is calling for thunderstorms until later tonight. You are more than welcomed to crash her until it clears up." Sean said as he stood up and walked into the kitchen "Have you eaten already?".

Just like him, Shelia thought always making sure she was taking care of herself. She looked at the clock on his microwave and noticed that it was just before 1 pm. She had eaten breakfast that morning before heading to Terry's, that was three hours ago. "Yes, I had breakfast earlier, so I'm not hungry. What movie were you thinking of putting on?" She kicked her shoes off and made herself more comfortable on his oversized couch.

She had to admit for a bachelor, he really knew how to decorate his home in such a way that it was inviting, cozy and modern. She was in love with his couch, and she loved how he used neutral tones in his furniture to draw your attention to his hanging artwork.

"I was thinking we could catch up on the Walking Dead series." He knew she hated gory shows, and before she could reply she saw the tease in his face as he laughed "Just kidding, did you want to watch the next episode of Greenleaf?" She smiled and replied, "Yes, how far along in the season are you? I finished season 2 already. Wait, I thought you said a movie?"

"You finished season 2 without me? So, what happened between Bishop and Rochelle? I figured we could start with a series then see how the storm moves."

"No spoilers from me. We can watch it again, I don't mind, besides I may have missed something. Do you have some chips and dip? The weatherman never knows what's going on, this morning there was only a 20% chance of rain."

"Chips are in the cabinet and the dips in the fridge door.

That's because you relay on your weather app to tell you the weather. Would it hurt you to turn on the weather channel every once in a while?"

She got up off the couch and walked into the kitchen, "Who needs the weather channel when you have Siri at your beckon call?" She giggled while grabbing the chips from the cabinet and looking in the refrigerator for the dip, then it suddenly hit her. This was what she wanted from Terry. The relationship her and Sean had was perfect, someone that she could just hang with, watch movies and not have to think about the next move with. No judgement, just someone she could relax with, chill with, enjoy life with. A friend.

She couldn't remember the last time her and Terry had been friends. What happened to them? When had they drifted so far apart? As she allowed her thoughts to wonder about Terry, she also considered the thought of whether or not she could have more with Sean. Could her and Sean be more than just friends? She had never considered it before, but now she was single. Could he be exactly what she was looking for in a relationship? No, she wouldn't even let her mind go down that path; besides, Sean was like a big brother to her.

When she stood up from the refrigerator, she noticed Sean was watching her. It wasn't just that he was watching her, but how he was looking at her. The way he looked at her now was definitely different from all the other times he had looked at her. She couldn't deny that his eyes seemed to draw her closer to him. The intensity in his eyes caused her skin to tingle. She felt a chill.

"You ok" she asked. She noticed how breathless she sounded as she walked towards the couch.

"Yea I'm good" he said breaking the eye contact that she hadn't noticed they were holding. She had always thought Sean was attractive, the way his chocolate skin highlighted his gorgeous smile had always made her blush, but now his smile was causing her body to react in a way that she couldn't ignore. He chose that very moment to flash her another one of his winning smiles, and her knees became so weak that she was glad she had already begun to sit down. "So Greanleaf? Or did you want to see what else the good Netflix had to offer?" he asked. "Greanleaf is fine with me, unless you wanted to watch something else?" she replied while opening up the dip. She told herself not to look at him. She realized that as long as she didn't look in his general direction, she could ignore how his shirt sleeves fit snuggly around his biceps and how his lips called to her for a soft kiss. As long as she kept her eyes focused on the chips and dip, she was fine, but she didn't know how to ignore how attractive he smelled to her at that moment, or even how to ignore how deep and husky his voice sounded as he commentated on the tv show.

"Did you want a throw? I turned the air conditioner off, but I think the storm is bringing in cold weather." Why was he so considerate? Especially now, when she was trying to ignore him and focus on the tv show.

"No, I am fine. I think I am going to head out as soon as this episode ends, it sounds like the rain is slowing down" She was lying of course, in the last fifteen minutes the rain had actually started falling harder and she even heard thunder in the distance, but the longer she stayed there the harder it was to ignore how comfortable his arms looked. She was also getting chilly, but the thought of crawling under a blanket while on his couch just caused her mind to wonder down a path, she wasn't ready to walk down.

"Slowing down, are you sure? It sounds like its picking up. You are welcome to ride the storm out here."

"No, I need to get home. Especially before it gets dark, I don't want to be trying to drive home at night in the rain."

He looked like he wanted to say something else, like he wanted to ask her to stay. She imagined what would happen if he asked her to stay. Would she say yes? She could already feel his lips on hers, his tongue trailing down her skin. She really needed to put some distance between him and her.

"You know, try to get ahead of the storm before it gets worse." She added just in case he was thinking of asking her to stay again.

He took a deep breath and shook his head. She couldn't read his face. It was as if he was battling with himself about something. That's when she knew. He knew exactly what she was thinking right now, how badly she wanted to come sit next to him, allow him to hold her and kiss her. That was typical Sean, it was as if he could read her mind. Maybe she should have been putting all the energy she had been trying to put into Terry, into a relationship with Sean. She couldn't think that way now though.

She stood up and walked to his front door. "I am going to

head home, try to clear my mind of somethings." She paused. "A few months ago, you told me that I needed to take some time for myself," she hoped that she was making sense to him, "I don't know if you were right, but I will give your suggestion some thought. Take some time for me and get me together."

"Ok, but Shelia is everything ok? I mean be honest with me."

She couldn't answer that question because she couldn't lie to him again, so she just shrugged and smiled. Before she changed her mind and decided to stay, she opened the door and ran into the rapidly falling rain.

She looked back as she opened her car door to see Sean standing in his front doorway watching her leave.

CHAPTER FIVE

She pulled up in front of her apartment building. The rain had picked up tremendously after she left Sean's, and she had even had to pull over a few times when the rain was too thick for her to see in front of her. What was usually a twenty-minute drive, had taken her 45 minutes. It may have been a bad idea to drive home, but she knew that staying at Sean's would've definitely been a challenge that she wasn't yet ready to accept.

She sat in her car watching the rain, when it showed no signs of slacking up, she turned her car off and took a deep breath. She was going to have to make another run for it. The short run from Sean's house to her car had left her wet and her clothes were still damp. She knew that from her car door to her apartment door was going to leave her soaked.

She stared at the apartment building, it saddened her to be coming home. She wasn't sure why, but the thought of spending the night alone, and not with someone, was something she dreaded. She desperately wanted to be held. Maybe she should just drive back to Sean's. That was ridiculous, she had barely made it home without an accident, she knew going back was too dangerous.

The rain seemed to fall harder as she reached for the car door handle. She saw dark clouds in the distance and knew that the thunderstorm was getting closer. She grabbed her purse and keys, opened her car door and while closing it behind her made a dash for the awning in front of her apartment door, pressing her key fob as she ran to lock her car doors. Thank God she lived on the bottom floor.

Once she was out of the rain and standing on her front steps, she took a deep breath, unlocked and opened her front door. She was met by Meowie her super fluffy and extra loyal cat. As soon as she saw him, her eyes lit up. How could she stay upset, sad, or lonely, when that big old ball of fur was always so happy to see her? She wasn't sure why cats always got a bad rep with non-cat owners, she knew her Meowie to be the most lovable and caring animal she had ever owned.

Meowie was the one constant in her life. He was a gift from her mother when she was a junior in High School, and since she had received him, he was always there when she needed him. From her first breakup in high school, to her moving into her own apartment after college. He had been there through it all. Even when she screamed and yelled, when she broke down into crying fits, and even when she threw dishes, she knew Meowie would never leave her. No, Meowie was loyal and dependable not like the other man in her life.

"Hi Meowie, did you miss me? Are you hungry?" He purred while rubbing up against her damp pants leg.

"Meow, meow" he purred, she took that to mean that yes, he was hungry, and yes, he had missed her.

"Oh Meowie, mama missed you too, let me tell you about the day I had."

This was what she needed most right now. A listening ear. She knew that Meowie wouldn't respond to her, but just being able to vent to him helped her to gain clarity about the events of the day.

———

"...and I actually showed up at his apartment this morning thinking he would finally give me some answers. I mean yes, I want answers, I mean what woman doesn't want and need answers especially after ten whole years. And why shouldn't Terry be willing to give me those answers. I mean if anything Terry owes me a reason why..." She paused.

In the middle of her rant, she heard herself. What was she saying, Terry owed her?

"Wow, Meowie am I really that stuck on Terry?"

"Meow"

She had been standing in her apartment kitchen for who knows how long holding Meowie's bowl of food. She hadn't even taken off her wet clothes.

She considered that maybe Sean was absolutely right. She really did need to take some time for herself, and to figure out her feelings.

"Damn Meowie what's wrong with me?"

"Meow"

She chuckled "You sound just like Sean, and you're right. I do need to just take some time to figure me out." She sighed, "I just need to take a deep breath, pause for a few minutes, and focus on nothing right now. There is time tomorrow to try to figure out this mess of a life that I am living."

Meowie purred as she finally placed his bowl of cat food down on the floor.

After filling up his water bowl, she walked into her bedroom, took off her wet clothes and laid across her bed. She felt the tears running down her face but instead of rushing to wipe them away she let herself cry once again. While listening to the storm outside, she laid there and wept, not thinking of Terry and not thinking of Sean, and she felt more at peace than she had in years.

CHAPTER SIX

He hadn't wanted to call her again, but he was worried about her. It had been a few weeks since she had left his apartment and he hadn't received a call or text from her. That was not typical of her. She would always call or text him at least once every few days.

On one hand he was happy he hadn't heard from her; on the other hand, he was really concerned. She had seemed very emotional the last time he had saw her, and he didn't want to think the worse, but he was concerned that she might be depressed or something. He had watched enough Lifetime movies to know that after bad breakups, women generally fell into a deep depression, and he wanted to make sure Shelia was ok.

The phone rang a third time and then the voicemail picked up.

"Hi this is Shelia, leave a message." Beep.

"Hi Shelia, this is Terry, again. Look we haven't talked in a while, so I was just calling to check on you. Feel free to shoot me a text or give me a call back. I'm worried about you."

He hung up. He hoped she didn't take him calling the wrong way. He really was just concerned about her. He had asked a few of their mutual friends about her, but they were all so nonchalant in their reply to him. One friend even went as far as telling him to get over her and move on with his life. He was over her, why couldn't everyone just see that he was concerned about her well-being. For chrissake they had dated for ten years, wasn't he allowed to be concerned about her.

What if she had hurt herself or what if someone had hurt her? He had tried to push the thought of her hurting herself out of his mind, but whenever he laid down to go to bed, he lost sleep from worry. What if she wasn't working or taking care of herself? He hated to imagine her in a depressed state, but he knew that that was often the case when people were forced to leave long term relationships. He couldn't understand what was so hard about her texting him back just to let him know she was ok.

He couldn't remember the last time they had gone this long without talking and it honestly didn't feel right. How can you go from talking to someone daily to ignoring their calls and texts? Hadn't their relationship meant anything to her, wasn't she the one that was at one point fighting to stay together, and now she goes weeks without even a hi. He had unfriended her on social media when he had ended the relationship, now he wished he hadn't because then at least he could see what she was doing thru her Facebook page. Her social media had always been private, and when he had sent her another friend request, she didn't even respond to it.

He decided to drive by her house again today. The last few times her car hadn't been home. If he could just see her to make sure she was ok he knew he would feel better.

He knew he sounded compulsive, but he really just needed to see her, or maybe even just hear her voice.

———

Shelia smiled.

She hadn't talked to her good friend Lisa in a while and the lunch date that they had just enjoyed was coming to an end. She leaned in for another hug. "Gosh, it was so good to see you. I hadn't realized how long it had been since we had last talked."

Lisa replied as she hugged her back "Girl yes, don't be a stranger, and let me know if you can make it next week."

"I will let you know as soon as I check my work schedule." Shelia said while packing up her purse to head back to work. She was in the middle of preparing for a job interview that could help set her up for a more permanent position at her job. The promotion was long overdue, and she kicked herself for not applying for it years ago. "Tell Larry and the kids I said hello and I will call you later"

"You better call me girl and remember take it one day at a time. I love you."

"I love you too. Thanks for the talk I really needed it."

Shelia blew Lisa another kiss, and as she walked away, she turned her thoughts to the possibility of picking up more responsibility at work. It always made her smile when she thought about the strides her life had taken in such a short period of time.

Over the last two months, she had reconnected with a few close friends, been given the opportunity to apply for a new position within her company, and she had even strengthened the bond between her and her Mom. She could honestly say she was happy.

She couldn't lie though, she thought about Terry often, a lot actually, but she knew that what they had was gone. At that moment she felt her phone vibrating. She pulled it out of her purse and noticed it was another call from Terry.

Why couldn't he get the hint? She was happy now, finally focusing on her.

She declined his call once again and promised herself that tonight she was going to finally block him.

CHAPTER SEVEN

"Hi, a group of us are thinking of going out for dinner Friday night. Still haven't set a time or location yet, but are you in?" Sean hit send on the text message and went back to working on sanding down the coffee table. His weeklong vacation from work was coming to an end and he could honestly say that he was glad that this home improvement was almost complete. He gave himself an imaginary pat on the back and continued to sand.

He felt his phone vibrate in his shirt pocket.

"Count me in and let me know the details later. My vote goes to sushi :-)"

Sean read the text from Shelia and was happy to hear she would be able to make it Friday night. She was working longer hours lately, waiting to hear back about a promotion at work, and he missed hanging with her. He was proud of her though, and he enjoyed every moment they were able to steal away together. He couldn't deny that he had feelings for her, but he also knew that she was coming out of a really serious relationship.

A few weeks ago, he had thought about mentioning the idea of them possibly dating, and although he wanted to see what could become of a committed relationship with her, he knew that it was bad timing. When they had first became friends, they had decided to keep their relationship strictly platonic, and he knew that right now, even though things with her and Terry were officially over, wasn't the time to pursue anything physical with her. He knew he was in love with Shelia, but he also knew what it was like to be hurt. He knew that the healing process, especially from a long-term relationship, could sometimes take years.

He had told Shelia that he would continue to be there for her as a friend, but he didn't promise her or himself that he would wait for her to heal. Although he loved Shelia, he knew that relationships came and went but that ultimately, he had to do what made him happier, so if he met someone else, he would pursue that relationship, but still offer his friendship to Shelia. If she wanted it that was.

"Awesome, I will add you to the group text"

After adding her to the group chat, he threw his vote in for a bar and grill and went back to working on the coffee table. If he could finish it this afternoon, he could revisit swapping out his bathroom faucet for a newer one. He knew that replacing the faucet would also require him to switch out the copper pipes and he just didn't know if he had the energy to give to that project right now.

———

Shelia sat down at her cubicle desk and pulled up the PowerPoint slides she had been working on before lunch. She quickly found herself distracted from her work. She found it hard to focus on her power point presentation and she didn't know why. Was it the text from Sean about dinner Friday night? No, she knew it wasn't that. It had to be the call from Terry, or maybe the stress from waiting on the results from the interview.

She knew in her gut that it wasn't the job interview, she had spoken with her supervisor earlier and she had learned, that not even taking the interview into consideration, based off her current work ethic she was top pick for the position, so she knew exactly what was distracting her. It was the notification for one voicemail on her cell phone. She wanted so badly to listen to it, just like she had listened to all the others. Terry's pleas for her to call him. The sad part is, she actually considered calling him. She had stared at his contact information on her iPhone on several occasions and debated with herself about calling him. After two months he still had an effect on her. Why couldn't he just stop calling her? If he would forget about her, then maybe she could forget about him. She feared that he would never stop calling, he had even been asking some of their mutual friends about her. Now after all that she had asked of him, all the begging she had done, now when she was finally healing, he starts trying to push his way back into her life.

She picked up her cell phone and unlocked it. She went to the phone app and hovered over Terry's number. Why hadn't she blocked him? It had been two entire months since they had last talked, and over five months since they had broken up. She hit the information button on his number, scrolled down and hit block. Then she deleted his contact information. Before she could think about it, she went to her call log and deleted all her recent phone calls, then she went to her voicemail and deleted his voicemail without being read. She even deleted all his old voicemails that she had played over and over the last few months. She took a deep breath and tried to remember if there were any other forms of communication between him, she needed to delete. She knew that know, before she changed her mind, and in order for her to move on, she had to get him out of her life.

She stared at the phone and thought, why not just change her number…yes, she thought that was exactly what she would do. She hadn't had a new number since before college, and it was time for her to make some much-needed changes in her life. She was happy with the thought of a new phone number and knew that this way there would be no way for Terry to contact her.

She thought to herself, might as well take it a step further and pick up the newest iPhone. With a smile, she was able to finally turn her attention back to the power point presentation in front of her. She needed to finish the presentation in order to work on another project that was due tomorrow morning. She knew that the promotion was hers, but at the same time she needed to wrap up any loose ends at her current position. She smiled from how proud of herself she was.

CHAPTER EIGHT

Terry pulled up to Shelia's apartment, he couldn't remember what hours she worked, but he thought maybe he would catch her at home tonight. It was Friday, and generally when he had driven by on Fridays her car was never in her parking spot.

He was shocked to see her car there on this particular Friday night. He had figured she would have been out living the single life or making deliveries for her Waiter job. He didn't intend to stop, but once he saw her car, he knew he needed to see her. He pulled his car up beside hers, in what used to be his parking spot, parked his car, turned off the engine and checked his face in the mirror. He hesitated before opening his car door. He hadn't seen her in over two months, and he wasn't sure if he would be welcomed by her, but he needed her to understand why he had made the decision to end their relationship. He felt that if he could make her see how the decision he had made was for the best, that maybe then he could move on. He also needed to make sure that she was moving on without him, and that she hadn't fallen into a state of depression. He got out of his car and walked up to her apartment and knocked.

After a short moment, he heard her reply "Who is it?"

"It's Terry." He answered while admitting to himself that she sounded happy. He paused and waited for her response. When she didn't respond he said "I need to talk to you. Please. If you have a second. Just to try to clarify somethings."

"What do you want Terry? What do you need to clarify?"

"I just want to talk. I have been worried about you. I called and never received a response and then a few days ago, when I called the system said your number was no longer active. Can you open up so we can talk? I just want to talk." He waited and was shocked when he heard the bolt lock release on the door. Then slowly the door was opened.

"Hi Shelia, I missed you."

CHAPTER NINE

She couldn't believe he was here. Somewhere in the back of her mind, she heard "Close the door now", but her arms wouldn't move. She was so confused. Just five minutes ago she had been applying her makeup to head to the bar and meet up with Sean and a group of friends, now she was staring into the eyes of the man she had loved with her entire being for all of her adult life.

"What did you say?" She asked, curious to see if he would repeat the words she had just heard. She had to admit that the thought of him missing her didn't quite move her the way she thought it would have. She was really confused by his words. How could he miss her? Wasn't he the one that had broken things off with her?

"I meant; I was worried about you, and I just wanted to make sure you were ok." She looked at him now, standing in front of her looking just like he had the last time she had seen him. She was definitely still attracted to him; even now she couldn't deny the physical attraction between them. As he stood there in front of her, she realized that maybe that was all there was, just a physical attraction. She didn't feel that heart tug she had once felt anymore. She also realized what he had just said, he hadn't said he had missed her, he said he was worried about her. Worried about her? What did that mean?

"Well, I am fine. Can I help you with anything else?". She wanted him gone. The longer he stood there, the angrier she became, how dare he pop up at her home and question whether or not she was ok. As if to say, that without him, she would be a bumbling wreck. Who did he think he was, some kind of god?

"No, I just…. I mean…are we good? I hadn't heard from you, and I just…I mean…are you angry? I mean, can we talk? I just figured I could try to explain why I think we need to be apart…"

She couldn't believe what she was hearing. Was he rambling? She couldn't deal with this now. After two months she was finally feeling happier, and now he shows up. To do what, finally answer the questions she had been asking. She took a deep breath; she didn't want to be angry not tonight. Tonight, was a night of celebration, she wanted to be happy, and she wouldn't let him ruin this night for her. She had just received news that she was accepted for the promotion. This meant that not only would she be receiving more responsibility, but she would also no longer be an hourly employee; her new position was a salary job. Of course, she would sometimes be required to work longer hours, but she felt that she was up for it. On top of her good news, her mom was headed up in two days to spend a few weeks with her. This would be the first time her mom had ever been to her apartment. So yes, she had been in a really good mood. That was before she had opened her front door.

"Look Terry, I am good. As for us, there is no us. You were right. We are both growing in different directions. Thanks for checking on me, but it wasn't necessary. I have to go." She looked him into his eyes, pausing to make sure there wasn't anything between them left unsaid. She wasn't nervous, or angry. At that moment all she felt was peace. She used to love to stare into his beautiful dark eyes, she remembered how she used to always search them for signs of whatever emotion he was filling, this time she didn't though. She didn't check for his emotions; she didn't gaze off and try to think of what to say next. She knew exactly what to say next, and she could care less what he was feeling right now.

"Goodbye Terry." She didn't whisper or shout, she simply said it. Just like she would have said it to a stranger she had just met. Then she closed the door and smiled.

At that moment she realized that whatever he did was his choice. She couldn't make him be with her and she couldn't make him love her. Even if she could, why would she want to be with someone that had to be forced to be with her? She took a deep breath, closed her eyes and smiled. She then went back into her bathroom and finished applying her eye liner. Once she was done with her makeup, she checked her outfit in the mirror one last time and headed out to meet up with her friends.

When she opened her front door, Terry was no longer standing on her front porch. She took one quick look around and headed to her car while typing up a text.

"On my way, first round of drinks on me in celebration of my promotion!"

Hitting send she thought to herself, yes, ten years was a long time, but it was not an eternity.

CPSIA information can be obtained
at www.ICGtesting.com
Printed in the USA
LVHW111142220621
690838LV00007B/88/J

9 781664 176898

TEN YEARS
AND NOTHING

Library of Congress Control Number:		2021910636
ISBN:	Hardcover	978-1-6641-7689-8
	Softcover	978-1-6641-7688-1
	eBook	978-1-6641-7691-1

Print information available on the last page.

Rev. date: 05/26/2021

To order additional copies of this book, contact:
Xlibris
844-714-8691
www.Xlibris.com
Orders@Xlibris.com
828845